This book belongs to
Caitríona

~~Caitríona~~

LOVE
Ruth ♡

Children's
POOLBEG

THE COW
WATCHED THE
BATTLE

A Paperback Original
First published 1990 by
Poolbeg Press Ltd.
Knocksedan House,
Swords, Co. Dublin, Ireland.

© Marjorie Quarton 1990

ISBN 1 85371 084 9

This book is published with the assistance of
The Arts Council/An Chomhairle Ealaíon, Dublin.

Cover design by Steven Hope
Illustrations by Steven Hope
Typeset by Print-Forme,
62 Santry Close, Dublin 9.
Printed by The Guernsey Press Ltd.,
Vale, Guernsey, Channel Islands.

THE COW WATCHED THE BATTLE

MARJORIE QUARTON

Children's
POOLBEG

Contents

The Cow Watched the Battle

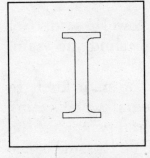n the morning, the sun rose behind the mountains and the cock crowed and wakened the man.

The man rose from the hearth where the woman lay sleeping. He stretched himself and yawned. He was tired. Then, stooping under the low doorway, he went out into the morning. The child followed him.

Then the man and the child walked down the mountainside in the dew to the place where the cow was. The cow lay on the hillside. She chewed her cud. She thought her own thoughts.

The child looked away down the mountainside, down from Tountinna to Lough Derg, where the sun touched the water.

The child asked, "Where do those boats come from? What men are those at the Look-Out?"

The man spoke to the cow. He said, "Get up, will you." To the child he said, "Whisht."

The cow got up and the man knelt to milk her. She gave little milk. She swung her tail which was long and twisted at the end, and struck the man on the side of the face.

The child said, "The boats are coming to the land. I will go down."

The man spoke to the cow. He said, "Ah, you are not worth milking." To the child he said "Come back outa that. Hold the cow's tail."

The man finished milking and the cow turned her head and looked where the child looked. She saw a thousand armed men at the Look-Out. She turned away and drank at the spring.

The man went home with the milk and the child went with him, looking back.

The sun rose higher in the sky and it grew warm. Many flies came and settled on the cow. She swished her tail as she ate the sweet herbs on the hillside.

The boats drew in to the lake's edge under the mountain. There, the men at the Look-Out could not see them. The men waited in silence.

The cow ate the sweet herbs. She thought her own thoughts. The flies troubled her.

The men at the Look-Out sat down and rested, except for one who watched.

The sun approached the centre of the sky, and the flies buzzed around the cow. She went to seek a shady place.

The men from the boats gathered at the low road below the Look-Out. They were a great army.

The cow lay down in the shade. She blinked her eyes and turned to lick her shoulder with her long, rough tongue. She thought her own thoughts.

The watchman exclaimed, pointing downwards. The men from the boats climbed into view. They were panting and the sun shone in their eyes and glinted on their helmets.

The men at the Look-Out waited in silence. They wore no helmets.

The cow lay on the mountainside. She lay in the shade because the flies troubled her.

The sun passed its height and the heat of the day grew less.

The men from the boats came on. Then the men at the Look-Out attacked the men from the boats with a yell, with knives and swords and spears. The men from the boats fell back, but did not turn to run.

The cow lay on the hillside; and the cow watched the battle.

The men from the boats advanced more slowly. They waved their spears and yelled their defiance. The men from the Look-Out were fresh; they had climbed no mountain. But they had no helmets.

The cow lay on the hillside; the cow watched the battle.

Two thousand men fought with swords

and spears and knives. Their battle-cries echoed from Tountinna across to Scariff, and from Killaloe in the south to Portumna in the north.

The cow lay on the hillside. She chewed her cud as she watched the battle.

The battle raged for two hours. Seven hundred men lay dead or dying. Their blood stained the green grass.

The cow lay on the hillside; she thought her own thoughts. As the sun moved towards the west, the flies troubled her less. She left the shady place and cropped the sweet herbs.

Then the men from the boats turned and fled back the way they had come. The men from the Look-Out followed them, yelling their triumph.

The cow watched their flight. When she had eaten her fill, she lay down. She listened to the groans of the wounded.

Many fell on the mountainside as they ran. Those who still lived rowed away in their boats.

At sunset, the man came and milked the

cow; the child was not with him. "Ah," said the man, "you are not worth milking." The cow swished her long, twisted tail and struck him on the ear.

When the man had gone, the cow drank at the spring. It grew dark. She lay down. She thought her own thoughts.

The Story of the First Greyhound

undreds of years ago, there were no grey-hounds in Ireland. Ireland without greyhounds! It was like potatoes without salt, or bacon without cabbage.

There were wolfhounds for hunting the wolf.

Deerhounds for hunting the deer.

Foxhounds for hunting the fox.

Boarhounds for hunting the boar—but there were no greyhounds at all.

The people who lived in Ireland long ago did not realise what they were missing. They had never seen a greyhound, so they could not miss them.

One fine day in harvest time, a rich

young man called Terence rode through
Nenagh on his way to Dublin. He was
guided to the town by the tall keep of the
new castle, then he turned westward and
crossed the great fair green which gave
the town its name. There, he saw some
boys cruelly beating a mongrel dog. The
dog howled pitifully, and Terence, who had
a kind heart, turned his horse and put the
boys to flight.

The dog, which stood as high as the sole
of Terence's boot as he sat on his horse,
was lean, mangy and yellow-eyed. Its legs
were long, and so was its tail, which was
tucked in against its empty belly.

"Go home," said Terence, for he did not
know that the dog had never had a home.
He turned his horse's head in the direction
of Toomevara and trotted away.

Now Terence was a wealthy young man,
and had all he needed in the way of horses,
dogs and fine clothes.

He loved to dress in bright colours, and
it was said by some that he washed
himself all over every week. He could not

bear any but clean linen next to his skin, and was commonly held by his servants to be mad. Likewise, he would not keep a horse unless it was sound and handsome. It must be free from blemishes and be young and swift.

Terence owned some of the finest deerhounds in Ireland, and they too were beautiful. They were savage it is true, with all but Terence, but they were the fastest and handsomest dogs in the province of Munster. If one of his dogs was mauled in a fight, Terence could not bear to have it near him until its wounds were healed.

As Terence rode down the hill to Roscrea, where he was to change his horse, he chanced to look round, and saw that the dog was following him—the same long-legged mangy cur that he had befriended in Nenagh. Terence turned his horse with the intention of driving it away, but then he thought, it will abandon the chase when I have a fresh horse. Already, it has run seven leagues.

Terence was travelling to Dublin to meet the young lady he was going to marry. Her name was Gráinne, the daughter of a rich merchant, and she was said to be as beautiful as she was wealthy.

The following day, as he rode through Monasterevin, Terence looked round and saw the dog still following; footsore now, and a long way behind. Poor brute, thought Terence, and rode on. By nightfall, the dog was no longer in sight.

It was then, as he crossed the Curragh of Kildare in the twilight that Terence was attacked by bandits. He fought them bravely, but they were many and desperate. They took his horse, and stripped him of his money belt and jewellery. They dared not kill him, for they feared his father's revenge. So they tied his hands and feet, and melted away into the night with his sword, his horse and his purse.

Terence did not know how long he lay in the darkness, with the first frost of autumn chilling him to the bone. He groaned, for the cords that bound his wrists and ankles chafed him sorely.

At length, he felt a warm dampness on his hand and, in the light of early dawn, he saw that the dog was licking blood from his fingers. For many hours it lay by his side, then all of a sudden, it got up and gazed into the distance, its ears lifted. Then it set off at a furious pace, and Terence thought, my last friend has deserted me.

It was not so. The dog had sighted a hare and coursed it until it caught it, killed it and began ravenously to eat it. Then it bethought itself, and began to drag what remained of the carcase towards Terence.

"Thank you, my friend; I haven't come to that," said Terence. "Eat it yourself." The dog did as it was told, and returned to lie beside Terence.

The same day, a band of young men set out from Dublin to meet Terence. They supposed he had lost his way, and they cantered across the Curragh, riding the finest of horses and dressed in their best.

They were of the bride's family, and were as fond as Terence of hunting and finery. With them, they had two enormous wolfhounds with jewelled collars.

Terence had fallen into an exhausted sleep, and they might well have failed to see him lying among the gorse bushes had not the dog raised its voice in the most piercing of howls.

In little time, the young men had cut Terence's bonds and heard his story.

"And what is that pray?" asked one of them, pointing a scornful finger at the long-legged dog, crouched shivering, licking its paws.

Terence looked at his friend with new eyes. He looked past the dirty, verminous coat to the faithful heart beneath. What should he say? It was a grey dog, so he said, "He is a greyhound."

"It is the first 1 have seen, is it a new breed?"

"It is," said Terence. "It is the newest and the rarest breed of all. His name is Finn." With that, he gave his friend the finest name he could think of.

Finn had many sons and daughters and, because there was none likes him, they came in many colours. Some were black, some fawn, some brindled, some white.

But the first greyhound was grey.

The Poor Man's Heifer

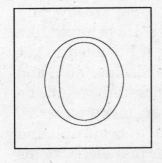nce, long ago, there was a rich man who lived in a castle on a fertile plain, not far from Thurles in the county of Tipperary. The lush grass grew right up to the outer defences of the castle, and the finest of cattle grazed within a bowshot of the grim arrow-slitted walls. In the distance lay the great brown bog, and beyond that, the blue hills.

The rich man had not worked for his wealth. His father before him had been not only rich, but grasping and heartless. He had fought battles and increased his domain. He had cared for nobody and had been hated by all. Even his wife had feared his rages. A delicate woman, she had died after her son, the rich man of our story, was born.

This rich man was not as wicked as his father had been. He was greedy and selfish, but without spite. He behaved like a spoiled child, sulking if he failed to get his own way. He was handsome, vain, and without thought for others. Above all, he was lucky. Lucky at war, lucky at cards, lucky in love. He had a beautiful and loving wife who lived for him alone, so his castle was a home as well as a fortress.

His luck held from one year to the next. When he was not feasting, fighting, or gambling with other rich men, his favourite occupation was riding. He rode about the countryside, splendidly dressed, his hawk on his wrist, mounted on a magnificent white horse named Ruairi.

Sometimes, he would ride along the track which crossed Littleton Bog, where it was almost impossible to make enough money to eat. There if he met a poor turf-cutter, he would stop his horse and laugh aloud.

"You poor creature," he would say, "you are killing yourself with work, when a little imagination could bring you riches." The turf-cutter would keep on digging without looking up. Best not to argue with the son of Blaise of the Iron Hand.

One day, the rich man was riding past a cottage on the edge of the bog, when he noticed a strawberry roan heifer, tied out on the roadside to graze. He stopped in surprise. This was the first beast he had seen since leaving his own estates, and he wondered how a man from the bog could afford such a fine heifer. He rode up to the cabin door, and asked the poor turf-cutter who lived there, "Will you sell me your heifer?"

"No sir," replied the poor man. "That heifer is all that I have in the world. I would sooner starve than sell."

The rich man tried arguments, persuasion and, finally, threats. All to no avail. At last he rode away in a rage. When he reached his castle, he mentioned the heifer to his steward. "I know the man," said the steward. "You should have offered him drink, for that is a thing he cannot resist."

Soon afterwards, the rich man returned to the cottage with a great leather flagon of the finest mead. This time, he told the poor man he was sorry for his behaviour and regretted his threats. "Come, let us drink on it," he said, and offered the flagon to the poor man, having first drunk himself.

"This mead is like nothing I have ever tasted," said the poor man in delight. "I should not be drinking, because I have not eaten. However..." He tilted the sheepskin to his lips again.

"Drink as much as you like," said the rich man, carelessly.

Soon the poor man became noisy, and began to boast about his heifer. "There is none like her in the counties of Tipperary and Kilkenny," said he.

"If that is the case, I will play cards with you," said the rich man. "Your heifer against my white horse Ruairi, which is famous from Fair Head to Mizen Head."

So they played, the rich man's luck held, and he won the game. The poor man came to his senses too late. He loosed his heifer and, weeping at his own folly, began to lead her towards Thurles.

The rich man rode on ahead, reached home and ate his dinner. Then he rode back along the way, and met the poor man and the heifer upon the road.

Now as he saw the lord of the castle riding towards him, carelessly sitting on his white horse and with his falcon on his wrist, the poor man's rage and despair overcame him. He took off his hat, dropped on one knee, and cursed the rich man, Up, Down and Across.

The rich man trembled with fear and returned to his castle. When his servants told him the heifer had arrived and had been added to his herd, he didn't reply. Within the space of a week, his strength had left him, and he took to his bed, where he lay, sick of a wasting disease, for a year.

Each day he craved milk to drink. His

parched throat was eased neither by water nor wine, and when mead was brought to him, he screamed out, "Take it away!" With dry lips, he gasped, "Milk! Bring me milk!" But when it was brought to him, he could not swallow it. He groaned and tossed about in his bed and when his wife tried to comfort him, he turned his face to the wall, so that she ran weeping from the room.

When he neared death, he sent for a servant, and whispered to him, "Give the poor man's heifer back to him."

This was done, and the servant returned to his master's bedside to tell him of it. He entered the room, and there lay the rich man dead, with a smile on his face

The Hairy Man

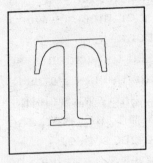

he Hairy Man lived in a cottage on the banks of the Newtown River. His name was Patrick, and before he vexed Old Kate of Carrigmadden, he was no hairier than you or I.

Patrick was a fine young man, tall and broad-shouldered. He had a head of curly, black hair, which he kept cut short. He wore no beard and shaved his face at least twice every week.

When Patrick was still young, both his parents were "carried off" by a fever, and he was left on his own.

One day, he walked down to the mill, and, for the want of anything better to do, he was helping to saw up logs. Not being used to the work, he laughed when the other men told him to take care. It wasn't long before he was in trouble. He reached across the saw for another piece of wood and cut his arm to the bone.

The woodmen were used to accidents, so they didn't worry too much about Patrick. They bound up his arm tightly with cloths, after washing the wound in the river, and told him to go home and get sense.

That night, when Patrick was in bed, he woke and realised that his arm was bleeding. He lighted a candle, and was horrified to see how much blood he had lost. His first thought was to fetch a doctor, but the nearest was in Nenagh. He had only his own two feet or the four feet of his donkey to take him there; he would bleed to death before he could get there.

Then he remembered a woman called Kate who lived in Carrigmadden. She was able to stop bleeding and had saved many lives.

"Maybe the cure will be worse than the disease," thought poor Patrick, "for they

say she is as ugly as the Devil himself,
with a temper to match."

Patrick set out to walk up through the
fields to Carrigmadden, and reached
Kate's house as the dawn was breaking.
She was up already and said to him—

"You are a fine young man, whoever you
are. What do you want with Kate?"

"My arm is cut. Can you keep me from
bleeding to death?" Patrick staggered and
sat down on a tree stump.

"Of course I can, me fine young man,"
replied Kate, and she laid her two dirty old
hands on the wound. Her fingernails were
as black as coal, and as she leaned
forward, her long greasy, grey hair
brushed Patrick's face.

Straight away, the blood stopped
flowing. Patrick began to thank Kate, but
she interrupted him and said—

"You don't like me, I can see into your
mind. I know everything: I dream about
things to come."

"I do that as well," said Patrick. "Thanks
for the cure; do you take money?"

"I do not, for if I did I would lose the power." The old woman was staring at Patrick. "What do you mean, you dream of things to come? Only I do that."

"Ah, go on," Patrick laughed at her. "I'll tell you something Missis. Look at the bare hills above. The day will come, and maybe not so far ahead, when all that will be forest again, as they say it was a thousand years ago. Coumroe and Curragh and Kilparteen will be all trees. I dreamed it."

Then Kate flew into a rage and she screamed out—

"Be off with you—you and your old dreams! I'll make you sorry for them!" She picked up the sweeping brush, and Patrick made off as fast as his weakness would let him.

When he got home, he washed his arm in the river, and there wasn't so much as a drop of blood coming from it.

Patrick thought "How hairy my arm is— I never noticed before."

Even as he watched, the hair on his arm

grew longer and blacker. He felt his chin—
he had two inches of beard. He glanced
up—he could see his own eyebrows.

In a panic, he ran and locked himself
into the house. By nightfall, he was
covered all over with hair, like a bear. He
cut it off and at once it grew again.

For days he didn't show himself out of
doors, living on potatoes and water. Then
a neighbour called, and ran away as if the
devil was after him.

Poor Patrick was dying for company,
and he had neither tea nor bread in the
house, so he chanced going down to the
pub in Newtown; but as he came in by one
door, the customers all fled through the
other. It was the same wherever he went.

In the end he went back to Kate and
begged her to end her magic.

"I will if you tell me what I want to hear,"
said Kate.

So Patrick said "You are the most
beautiful woman in all Ireland, and the
only one whose dreams come true. Mine
were nonsense."

Then the hair fell off him in a little heap, and Kate gathered it up to fill a cushion.

Patrick went home as handsome as he had been before, but Kate had not finished with him. If ever he thought anything bad about her—and it was hard to blame him—blood would ooze from the scar on his arm until he managed to think about something else.

The Wicked Harness Maker

any years ago, there lived in a Tipperary town a harness maker named Paddy Duffy.

Paddy was a good workman. His shop was usually full of collars, winkers and breechings, waiting to be lined or mended. He made common harness too, for asses and horses.

He seldom got the chance to make the harness used in those days for the carriage horses of the rich. Such harness would be made of the best leather, mounted with brass or silver plate.

The people who could afford to use harness like this would not employ Paddy because of his drinking, foul mouth and filthy shop.

At length, Paddy decided to take on an apprentice. In those days, apprentice boys went to work between twelve and fourteen years old as a rule, and had to serve seven years for their keep alone. If they ran away, they could be fetched back by the police.

The lad that old Paddy took on was a twelve year old called Tom. Tom was small and wiry, hard-working and eager to please. He found he was expected to clean the kitchen, bedroom and shop, as well as cooking Paddy's meals. All this and twelve hours a day in the shop, working and learning his trade.

Tom's fingers were not strong enough to push a needle through leather. As his meals consisted of bread and milk twice a day, he didn't grow any stronger. The high counter was above his shoulder, so he had to sit on it to work.

Old Paddy staggered about, wheezing and swearing. He abused Tom steadily, and hit him a dozen times a day, often on the face or on the head. This made Tom so nervous that his hands shook as he worked. One day, he was cutting thongs for bootlaces, when the trembling of his hand made him cut one in half.

With a shouted oath, Paddy lunged at him and struck him a blow which knocked him off the counter. Tom picked himself up off the floor and ran away. Out of the shop—up the street—but not far, for a policeman caught him and held him by the collar.

"Not so fast, my lad. Where are you going?"

Tom couldn't get away, so he begged— "Please don't take me back to Paddy Duffy, he has half killed me already."

The policeman said—"An apprentice, are you? Well young man, I'm sorry, but I'm obliged to take you back. It's the law."

So the policeman took Tom back, warning Paddy not to be too hard on the child.

As soon as he had gone, Paddy roared out—"You'll not run away again, you young devil. I'll mark you for my own!"

With that, he grabbed Tom and pierced his ear as if for earrings but with a much bigger hole, for he used an awl. Then he pushed a piece of copper wire through the hole and twisted it into a ring. Poor Tom cried in vain. Paddy said "Now try running away. That will keep you here and keep off the evil eye as well."

After a few days, Tom's ear turned septic and he began to feel ill. Paddy took fright, thinking the boy might die, and he sent him to the doctor. He took care to remove the wire first, and warned Tom to come back if he valued his life.

The doctor was busy, and handed Tom over to his housekeeper, who was a very strange woman indeed. She was supposed to be able to cure diseases as well as the doctor and she looked extremely odd. She was tall, thin and pale with blazing green eyes and red hair. From head to toe she was dressed in black.

When she saw the state of Tom's ear, she persuaded him to tell her his story.

"If I cure your ear," she said, "would you like to stay here and run errands for the doctor and me? You would be well fed and clothed, and you will get a little money besides."

"I would stay if I dared," said Tom, and so he did.

The next day, Paddy Duffy was in an extra bad temper. He had come in drunk as usual, and hadn't lit the open fire he cooked on. The shop was dirtier than ever.

As he opened his shutters, he saw a tall red-haired woman at the door. He opened it, and she greeted him pleasantly, saying "Tom, your apprentice, has blood-poisoning. He won't be back for a fortnight, so I have brought my nephew, Larry, in his place."

Larry was about fourteen, with curly red hair, freckles and bright blue eyes.

"I suppose I must make the best of it," grumbled Paddy; so the woman went away, leaving Larry in the shop.

"Out to the back and light the fire. Put on a pot of water to boil," ordered Paddy.

A few minutes later, smoke poured through into the shop. Paddy hurried out and found Larry stoking the fire with books and bundles of bills and receipts. He easily dodged the blow Paddy aimed at his head.

"Do you want to burn the house down?" roared Paddy. "Clear the table and boil the kettle!"

Larry tossed the kettle into the pot of boiling water. "It'll soon boil, I daresay," he said, and he swept everything off the table onto the floor with a crash.

Black in the face with rage, Paddy chased him round the room. Larry danced just ahead of him into the shop.

There he knocked over a big tin of saddler's tacks, which rained down all over the floor

Paddy was still in his slippers which had holes in them, so it wasn't long until he stepped on a tack. Again and again he lunged at Larry who dodged him every time, throwing the pieces of harness in Paddy's path and laughing loudly. He upset the pot of glue over the tacks on the floor, and tossed a ball of waxed thread through the door into a passing cart. He looped the end of the thread round the doorknob. and it kept unwinding until the farmer reached his home a mile away.

Beside himself with fury, and with the tack still fast in his foot, Paddy seized a heavy mallet and hurled it at Larry's head. Larry ducked, and the mallet crashed through the shop window, landing in a shower of broken glass at the feet of that same policeman who had returned Tom.

The policeman wasn't cruel and had been wondering how poor Tom had fared. He picked up the mallet and marched into the shop.

What a sight met his eyes! The floor was strewn with nails and rivets stuck fast in a pond of glue. Harness lay about everywhere, and Paddy, dancing with rage, was brandishing a blackthorn stick.

Acrid smoke rolled in from the other room.

"What's going on here?" demanded the policeman.

"Only let me catch that boy," gasped Paddy. "I'll murder him! I'll…"

"What boy?"

Both men looked around the shop. There was no boy to be seen, there or anywhere else in the house.

The policeman led Paddy away, far from gently, to the barracks, where it took him a long time to explain his behaviour. Only by promising to behave in future, and not to take on another apprentice, did he avoid being sent to the Magistrate or, worse still, the madhouse.

It took Paddy three days to clean up his house, and he found himself the laughing stock of the town, so he kept very quiet, and didn't tell his story to a soul.

The Fat Princess

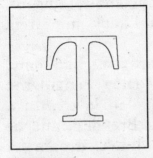 oday, there is no such thing as a fat princess. She may be delightfully plump, blooming or bonny. Six hundred years ago, there were fewer words to choose from. Princesses, like other mortals, were either fat or thin. Princess Maeve was fat.

It was arranged that she should marry the son of the ruler of Ulster. He, when, he saw her, broke his contract, and married a slender girl chosen by himself.

Naturally Maeve felt hurt, although she didn't care for the young man. Her mother, an unkind woman, was annoyed.

"We'll never get you married if you don't lose weight," she said. Maeve starved herself almost, but to no avail.

Her suitor from Ulster hadn't stayed long enough to find out what sort of person she was. Loyal, generous and intelligent, her sense of humour kept her from despairing.

By the time Maeve's parents had found another man whom they considered suitable, she had fallen in love with a young merchant called Brendan, and he with her. Brendan didn't dream of marrying a Princess. He thought about Maeve all the time and often wished they were married. Then he would pull himself together and dismiss his fancies as fairytales.

One day, the Queen said, "You are to be married to Fergus, brother of the King of Connacht. He is coming to visit us tomorrow and I don't want to hear any silly nonsense from you."

Maeve didn't like the sound of this. In those days, daughters never dreamed of arguing with their mothers. Maeve thought of Brendan and wept, but she said nothing.

Fergus arrived with great pomp the next day. Maeve was watching from an upper window of the castle as the retinue approached.

Who was that, riding at the head of the column? Surely not Fergus! He had an untidy thatch of greasy flaxen hair, a great drooping moustache, and only one eye. The wound which had removed the other had dragged a furrow down his cheek, which pulled his mouth crooked. He was fifty years old and looked sixty.

Horrified, Maeve turned to Brigid, her maid. "Who is that?" she asked with a shudder.

"That is Lord Fergus, from the province of Connacht," replied Brigid, with a pitying glance.

"Quick, Brigid! Lend me some of your clothes for a disguise. I must run away!"

Brigid laughed at her. "How could you wear anything of mine, Princess? I am half your size."

"I must dress up as a stout old dame

then," declared Maeve, and that is what she did. When she was dressed in the housekeeper's Sunday best, she looked very like a nun, in a long, loose black robe, with a kerchief hiding her curly brown hair. She had no difficulty in slipping through the crowd, and got a closer look at Fergus. Ugh! I'd rather jump into the Shannon, thought Maeve, trying not to break into a run.

She strolled along the country road with a basket on her arm until the castle was out of sight, then, gathering up her skirts, she jumped the ditch into the fields and never stopped running until she reached Brendan's house.

Brendan was dismounting from his horse at the door when, to his astonishment, a stout elderly woman in a long black robe hurled herself sobbing into his arms. Brendan, reeling under her weight, managed to support her, while restraining his startled horse with one hand. He began to say, "I think you mistake me for someone else," when

Maeve raised her bramble-scratched and tear-stained face.

"Maeve! Princess! What are you doing here?"

In a few moments, Maeve had told her story.

"What shall I do? At any moment my father's soldiers will arrive and take me back by force."

"Over my dead body!" exclaimed Brendan. "Quickly, mount my horse behind me, and we will escape together."

"If only," said Maeve, "we could reach Bunratty Castle, my uncle, the Earl, would protect me and you too."

"That is where we will go then."

Heaving the fat Princess onto the horse's back proved to be difficult. At last, Brendan had to lift her up first, then clamber onto his horse's neck, and from there to a more usual position for riding. At last, they were both seated on the alarmed and overloaded horse.

Maeve, who had vaguely expected Brendan to swing her up behind him and gallop away, was anxious about the delay. Thank God night was falling and the horse black. They would be hard to see.

It was twelve miles to Bunratty and a bog lay in the way, crossed by few paths, and those not known to many.

"It's lucky I was at Bunratty only yesterday," said Brendan. "I took some silks to show to the ladies, and I remember the pack road perfectly."

Maeve said nothing. She was uncomfortably balanced on the horse's back behind the saddle, and felt as if her teeth were being shaken out of her head.

As they trotted across the bog in the twilight, Brendan pointed ahead at a spreading thorn tree. "That is the lone thorn of Rath," he said. "We are on the right road. The road turns right here."

At that moment, Maeve heard a furious yell behind her. Looking round, she saw Fergus himself coming at full gallop on a great roan horse with a white face. She screamed aloud with fear, and clung to Brendan more tightly than before.

Brendan forced the black horse into a gallop, thinking every minute that Maeve would fall and pull him down with her. The horse, with his double burden, did his best, but the other gained on him at every stride.

As they reached the thorn, the roan horse was almost level with them. "Hold tight!" cried Brendan, and he pulled his horse as hard as he could to the right. The horse, perhaps remembering the road, answered the bridle. Fergus, who was spurring his horse forward with a slack rein, continued straight on.

Seconds later, horse and man were floundering in the bog. Two of Fergus's men, appearing through the dusk, were barely in time to pull up and go to his help.

"Fergus won't drown; his men will pull him out of the bog," said Brendan. "We must keep going as fast as we can."

At last, they reached the stream with its hump-backed bridge which formed part of the defences of Bunratty. Two men-at-arms had just ridden into the courtyard, and they swung their horses round, drawing their swords, when they heard Brendan's horse clattering after them.

"Don't harm us! It is I, niece of the Earl!" said Maeve, with what dignity she could muster.

Her uncle, the Earl, was extremely angry when he found that he was being asked to give sanctuary to the young merchant Brendan, as well as to his runaway niece. He told Maeve, who was tearfully pleading for help, to hold her tongue, and turned to Brendan.

"Young man, I think you had better explain yourself," he said grimly.

"Sir," said Brendan, "this young girl, your niece, was to have been married to Fergus of Connacht. You must know that, besides being more than twice her age, he is cruel and treacherous. I have traded in Connacht, and there they say that he murdered his first wife."

"Marry Fergus! Never!" The Earl was horrified at the idea. Evidently he knew nothing of it. He promised to do everything in his power to help the young people.

He was as good as his word, and persuaded Maeve's parents to make the best of things, and allow her to marry Brendan. The wedding was arranged for Easter.

Maeve began to talk of slimming so as to look her best for the wedding, but Brendan begged her not to.

"I love you as you are," he said. "And never forget, if you had been slim we would not have had the chance to marry."

As for Fergus, even his own followers hated him. The two soldiers hadn't tried very hard to save him. Weighted down by his armour, he had drowned in the bog.

The roan horse was luckier. The soldiers managed to pull him to safety, and took him back to Limerick. Good horses were scarce.

Manna from Heaven

In the famine times, when people were dying of hunger every day, but before the sickness came, Johanna was considered a very lucky woman. Usually, when a maid in one of the big houses married, she lost her job straight away, but not Johanna. Her employers had grown fond of her, and besides, her husband Mikey also worked at the big house, as a gardener. So the only difference was that Johanna walked home to the cottage in Ballydrennan Lane every evening. Johanna took home as much bread as she could carry in her apron for her young sisters and brothers, for she and Mikey were living with Johanna's

family.

One day, Mikey fell sick with stomach pains and a high fever. Johanna brought him milk and oatmeal from the big house, but in vain. After three days, he died, and was buried at Dromineer.

Now the family was in a sorry plight. Johanna was expecting a child, and the time came when she had to leave her work and go home. Soon, there was nothing left for the family to eat. A neighbour still brought milk from the big house, but there was no more bread or oatmeal. A girl working there was supposed to take food to the family twice a week, but she took them home to her own family instead.

One day, late in the summer, when Johanna was gathering old, stringy nettles to make broth, the priest called. He was thin and haggard like themselves.

"What will we do, Father?" asked Johanna.

The priest hadn't a notion, any more than themselves. He looked at the starving family, the children too weak even to cry. What could he say?

"Have faith," he said. "Remember how God sent manna to Moses in the wilderness, when he and his followers were starving."

"What is manna, Father?"

"Nobody knows," answered the priest. "It was white, we are told. Small white things, good to eat. It came from heaven while Moses slept, in answer to his prayers."

On Saturday, as she walked down Ballydrennan Lane with her sister Bridget, Johanna said, "We could do with some manna. I'm weak with the hunger, and the child will be born soon."

"Will we pray for it?" Bridget asked.

"I suppose we could. Things couldn't be any worse," said Johanna. "But I'm not getting down on my knees on the road. We'll go into the field."

In those days, the road ended at Fahy's house which is down now, just around the bend from Treacy's. After that, there was only a footpath, narrow and twisting, which joined the lane to the Dromineer Road. The footpath crossed the field below Carrig Hill, where Seymour's house is now. In that field, the sisters knelt to pray.

Johanna prayed, "Send us manna, oh Lord, for we are starving."

Bridget was much younger than Johanna—only thirteen. She had no faith in manna. She prayed, "Send us a good crop of blackberries, oh Lord, for we are starving."

They walked home, and the younger children were breaking up bread from the big house. "There's your manna," said Bridget, "white bread." But it was all gone in a minute—there was none left for Johanna.

At first light on the next day, Sunday, the hunger pains wakened her. She could sleep no more, so she got up. "I'll go and see were our prayers answered," she said to Bridget as she dressed, but Bridget was asleep.

Johanna went out. It was misty; soon it would be autumn. The grass was icy cold under her bare feet. She hurried along the footpath until she reached the field under Carrig Hill. As she came to the gap, she saw a small white thing, smaller than a baby's hand.

She cried out, "Thanks be to God, our prayers are answered!" and ran to look. There, shining with dew, was a mushroom. And another—and another! There were mushrooms all over the field. There, where mushrooms had never been seen before, they were coming up as Johanna watched. She filled her shawl with them, and hurried home as fast as she could.

From that day until the first hard frost, nearly two months later, the mushrooms never failed. The whole parish lived on them.

The strange thing is that, from that day to this, no more mushrooms ever grew in the field under Carrig Hill. God heard Bridget's prayers as well. There was the biggest crop of blackberries ever seen. That same autumn, the apple and pear trees were bent to the ground with fruit.

Johanna's child was born on the first day of October. In memory of the miracle of the mushrooms, she was named Grace.

The Electric Cat

The last witch in Ireland lived in a cave near the mouth of the Shannon. She was married to Michael, a beggarman who was almost always somewhere else. He hadn't wanted to marry her, but she put a spell on him and he had to.

The witch had a daughter called Shannon, after the great river. She was a bright girl, who would have liked to play with the children in the village at the top of the cliffs, but she wasn't allowed to. She used to steal up to the windows of the nearest house and peep in at the people inside, who were called Jerry and Kathleen Moran. Their son, Hugo, cycled

to school every day. He was about fifteen—
three years older than Shannon.

"Why can't we have a cooker, Mammy?"
asked Shannon, as she tried to light the
fire under the iron pot with damp
driftwood.

"Witches never have cookers," said her
mother.

"I wish you'd let me go to school."

"I can teach you more than any
schoolmaster."

"Please, Mammy, can't I have a bike?"

"Shannon! Whatever next? A cycling
witch? You will have my broomstick when
I die."

But Shannon didn't fancy the
broomstick. She used it for sweeping the
sandy floor, although it twisted in her
hands and sometimes squeaked and
whimpered. It didn't believe in tidiness.
One day, Shannon was polishing up the
rocky walls of the cave, instead of
searching them for spiders for the stock-
pot. The witch caught her at it, and
ordered her out of doors to collect frogs

and snails. "Anyone would think this was an ordinary house," she said.

"I wish we lived in a house with doors and windows," said Shannon. Then she noticed her mother's expression, so she took a can for the frogs and snails and ran off as fast as she could.

When Shannon had gone, the witch pottered about, mixing a vile-smelling brew on the fire and talking to herself. She was in a bad temper because her black cat had died and the cave was overrun by fieldmice. After what she had said to Shannon, she felt she shouldn't set a trap. Witches never set mousetraps.

She heard a step outside and went to see who was there. It was a black-haired lad with a tanned face and greenish eyes. "Who are you and what do you want?" demanded the witch.

"My name is Hugo Moran and I came to see Shannon," said the boy.

The witch gave him a wide friendly smile. "Come in, my dear," she said. "Shannon won't be long."

Hugo wasn't too keen to go in, but Shannon's mother didn't *look* like a witch. She wasn't old, and her hair was dark brown, not grey. True, she wore it loose, down to her waist, and it could have done with a shampoo and set.

"Come in, Hugo," she said. "Sit down by the fire."

The boy did as he was told.

It was evening when Shannon came home. She hadn't found any frogs and only about a dozen snails, so she expected a scolding, but her mother was all smiles.

"Where did you get the cat, Mammy?"

"He came to the door, dear. I asked him in, and he decided to stay."

"Isn't he handsome? What will we call him?"

"Tom," said the witch.

After supper, Shannon sat on the hearth, stroking the cat. His fur crackled and gave off blue sparks, but she was used to that sort of thing. As it got later, his eyes gleamed bright green in the dark, but when the witch stroked him, the glow changed to luminous red and his happy purr turned into a snarl. Red sparks ran fizzing up and down his back. "I wish you'd get an ordinary cat," said Shannon. "It might catch those mice."

The mice were scampering about, getting bolder all the time. Tom clouted the nearest with his paw, but made no attempt to pick up its body with his teeth.

"That cat is quite useless," said the witch next day. She was right. Tom sulked, refused to eat and allowed the mice to run over his paws. He walked up and down outside like a lion in a cage. It seemed as if he couldn't go beyond a certain point, about fifty yards from the mouth of the cave.

Late in the afternoon, a garda came looking for a missing boy called Hugo, whose bicycle had been found on the cliff path. Tom rubbed himself against the garda's trouser leg, purring hard, and showers of blue sparks filled the air. "My mother's out," said Shannon. "Don't mind those sparks—it's just magic."

"Magic? Nonsense, it's electricity. Cats are full of it," said the garda. But he didn't sound too sure about it, and was in a hurry to get back to his car.

When he'd gone, a thought occurred to Shannon. "Tom," she said, "Are you really a boy called Hugo?"

Tom miaowed and jumped about while his whiskers curled and uncurled and his eyes changed colour like traffic lights. "Stupid old magic," muttered Shannon. "Never mind—I'll think of something."

When the witch came home, Shannon had decided what to do. She told her mother that there was a law about going to school, and another one about living in a cave with a pile of bones outside it. "When the guard comes back I'll ask him about it," she said. "I'll be sent to school, and you'll be put in a house, or in a mobile home on a parking site."

The witch turned green with fear. "You wouldn't," she whispered.

"Yes I would, unless you turn Tom back

into a boy."

The witch laughed with relief. "Oh, if that's all..." she said. "I was going to do that anyway as soon as you were asleep. A more useless cat I never saw."

So Tom was turned back into a boy, and I'm sorry to say that he ran all the way home without waiting to thank Shannon.

Shannon was sure she would never see Tom again, but she was wrong. The garda had thought she was a clever girl, and he told the school inspector about her. Sure enough, later that year, she had to go to school. The witch was obliged to agree, because otherwise she would have been made to leave her cave and move into a house in the town.

Shannon and Hugo went to the Technical School, where Hugo learned to be a carpenter and Shannon learned to be a chemist.

When they grew up, they got married and had a baby boy. They decided to call him Tom.

The Lonely Snake

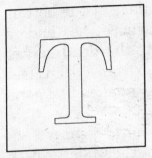

There are lots of stories which everyone knows but which aren't in the history books. They are called "legends," and are sometimes partly true and sometimes not. We all know the story about St Patrick driving the snakes out of Ireland: here is a tale about the only snake he overlooked.

The snake that St Patrick missed was about as long as your arm, with a pattern of green and brown diamonds along his back. He had a small three-cornered head with tiny little eyes and a forked tongue. His tongue flicked in and out, which frightened people and made them think he had poisonous fangs which he hadn't.

Even if he had been a poisonous snake, he probably wouldn't have bitten anybody, because he was never in a bad temper. He lived near the king's palace at the bottom of a dried-up well where he had a comfortable nest among the dead leaves. One evening, he woke up from a deep sleep to find that all the other snakes had gone. He was alone.

All night and all day for three days, the snake slithered about in the undergrowth, looking for his companions, his friends and relations. He couldn't call out to them—the only sound he could make was a hiss—but he knew the places where they used to meet and he tried them all. Nothing.

At last, feeling most unhappy, he crept back into the old well and fell asleep. When he woke, he had a good think, and decided he would have to make friends with some of the other wild creatures. But wherever he went, they fled.

The blackbird flew up off her nest shrieking with fear, warning all the other birds. The squirrels ran up trees and the rabbits down burrows, chattering with fright. Snakes like to eat small animals and birds' eggs, so this one knew in his heart of hearts that he was wasting his time. As the smaller creatures failed him, he tried talking to the goats and sheep that grazed near the palace. He wriggled towards them, smiling and hissing softly, with his forked tongue flicking in and out but they took to their heels.

In despair, he tried to make friends with the cattle and horses. The cattle stampeded with their tails in the air; the horses reared, swung round and galloped into the forest. The snake was alone again.

A snake has no friends, except for other snakes, he thought, as he dined off two fieldmice, washed down with milk. The milk had been spilt in the dairy when the cow spotted him and kicked the bucket over. The milkmaid, who hadn't noticed him sliding by, punched the cow in the ribs, picked up the bucket and got on with her work. The snake crept out through the drain, thinking that he might make friends with the milkmaid when the cow wasn't there, making a silly fuss.

People! Snakes don't eat people and people certainly don't eat snakes. He knew now—or thought he knew, where to look for some new friends. Holding his head high, he wriggled across the courtyard as fast as he could, up a rough piece of wall, through a glassless window with bars and down, down... He was in the palace cellar.

Directly over the cellar was the banqueting hall and there the king was eating and drinking with the ruler of a land far to the east. This visiting king had travelled all over Europe and as far as Asia. A native of a warm country, he was slim and dark, and was dressed in brightly coloured silk robes. He looked out of place in the Irish court, where the king and his friends wore short tunics and sandals. Big, powerful, with blond or red hair, the Irishmen looked what they were, skilled hunters and fighters. Their guest paid others to do his fighting for him.

As a present for the Irish king, the visitor had brought two slaves, captured in a town which he had conquered. They were twin boys, about fourteen years old, called Ali and Hassan. Their language was Arabic, and they had no idea what would happen to them. They huddled together on a bench, shivering in their thin silks, wide-eyed with fear.

The Irish king drank his wine and stroked his beard. He had a problem. He couldn't refuse the gift of the two boys— that would give offence and might even lead to war—but the last thing he needed was a pair of delicate looking creatures who could speak neither Irish nor Latin. He was sure they would be useless in the hunting field. He decided to give them to his daughter as pages.

The great jug of mead—strong wine, made from clover honey—was empty, and the king sent a servant down to the cellar for more. The servant found that the bung of the keg hadn't been properly tightened,

so a pool of mead had spilled on the floor.
With furtive glances to make sure he was
alone, he filled a mug and hastily drank it
off. Mead isn't a drink to be taken in
mugfuls and his head swam. He set down
the mug carefully and stared.

For a moment in the dim light, he
thought he saw a snake slithering away
into the shadows. But St Patrick had
banished all the snakes. He filled his jug
and stumbled up the steps. If he was
seeing snakes, he must be drunker that he
thought. He left the cellar door open.

The snake had drunk quite a lot of the
spilt mead on the cellar floor. It made him
feel sickish but brave. Even so, he
wondered how he would be greeted in the
dining hall. It was far too full of men, all
armed with sharp swords. He thought
perhaps he wouldn't try to make friends
with them after all.

Instead, he slipped unnoticed along the
wall, where the hangings hid him. When
he reached a flight of steps he climbed

them. The mead was making him feel cheerful but rather dizzy, so he went slowly. In the chamber above the great hall, he climbed up the side of the door and settled down on the stone lintel for a nap.

The snake woke with a start. A young girl with long reddish hair and a dress sewn with bronze coins had entered the room. A friend! A young friend with a kind, smiling face. He rapidly let himself down and rushed at her, hissing. The girl screamed and fled down the stairs. Forgetting to be careful, the snake slithered after her as fast as he could, begging her to wait for him in the only language he knew.

A moment later, he was dodging for his life as huge men swung sharp swords and heavy clubs. He dived under a bench where two dark-skinned boys dressed in bright silks were sitting together.

"Kill the snake!" yelled the men, but the foreign ruler went to stand with the two boys who cowered, sure that they were going to be killed themselves. "I saw the

snake," the ruler said. "It's not poisonous.
Let the boys keep it for a pet. They had one
in the marketplace where they were
captured, but it escaped."

Meanwhile, the boys got down and
looked under the bench where the snake
was hiding. Ali whistled a little tune while
Hassan waved his hand to and fro. Slowly,
the snake crept towards them—he had
found friends at last.

Some days later, a powerful chieftain
came to call on the king. He was known to
be bad-tempered and likely to pick a
quarrel with his host, so the courtiers
were racking their brains for some new
way of amusing him. The king's daughter,
who had been so terrified by the snake,
sang a number of songs while the harper
played all the tunes he knew. The great
chief sat scowling. He scowled harder
when the king's jester told some funny
stories about the people of Kerry, because
he had heard them all before, many times.

The king was wondering what he could

do next, when his daughter went and whispered in his ear. The king looked doubtful, but he agreed to send for the two new pages. Then Ali and Hassan entered the hall, clad in silks and jewelled turbans and carrying a basket. Ali sat cross-legged with the basket on his knee, playing on a pipe. The last snake in Ireland slowly uncoiled and reared up, weaving from side to side in perfect time with the music. Then Hassan lifted up the snake and draped him round his neck and arms. The great chieftain clapped, whistled and stamped; the king smiled.

The snake clung round Hassan's neck, hissing. His forked tongue flickered in and out. The dinner guests drew back, thinking that he was angry. They were wrong—he was laughing.

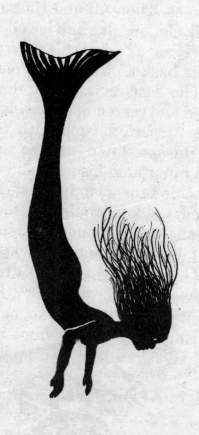

The Mermaid and the Postman

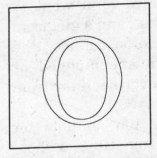

On the Kerry coast, not far from Dingle, lies a small sandy bay, shaped like a horseshoe.

There is a tiny village almost on the shore there, where the only buildings are the church, the school, the post office, the pub and three cottages, all clustered around at the end of the road which goes nowhere else.

The post office was kept by Mrs Finn, who had taken it over from her mother, who had taken it over from *her* mother. Mrs Finn had no daughter, but she had three sons. One lived in America, the youngest, Matt, was at school, and the middle one, Mick, was a postman. Mick tore around in his little green van all morning delivering letters, and in the evening he went fishing.

Then, one summer, Mrs Finn went to America to visit her eldest, and a girl from Tralee came to mind the post office. She was called Noreen and she laughed at Mick because he had never been far from home.

The sandy bay was too shallow for fishing with boats, but sometimes a shoal of bass came in, and all the local people went out to catch them. The time for this was when high tide came during the half hour between sunset and dark. When the word came, "The bass are in!" the men of the parish fetched out the long net which reached across the bay. The men, women and children waded into the sea in a long line, each carrying part of the net. When they were chest-deep in the water, they would drop the net, and wade back to land, pulling it through the water. Finally the strongest men would drag the net up the sand with its load of flapping fish.

Mick was almost late for the fishing. Noreen had got homesick and gone back to Tralee. He phoned her, but she said she wouldn't come back for anything. He ran down to the sea, and caught the very end of the net, next to his young brother Matt. Matt was ten years old, and he had red hair and although he was always cheerful, he was usually in some kind of trouble.

The net was dreadfully heavy. Mick and Matt tugged and tugged, and at last they saw there was a huge fish of some kind tangled up in the end of it. Up on the beach, the neighbours collected a big catch of bass, loading the fish into trailers for the market. It was getting very dark, and they had no light except the headlamps of a van parked up above the tide mark.

"Hey Mick! Will you roll up the net? We want to be going with the fish," shouted big Dan from Castlegregory.

"I will," said Mick, and he added, "Hush, you," to Matt who was jumping about in excitement. For Mick had seen a white hand sticking out of the net, and it was moving.

Mick and Matt stripped away the net, and first they came to a great scaly tail—bigger than the biggest salmon, then the tail joined the upper half of a girl's body, cold and white and slippery. Last of all, they pulled the net clear of her face. She had wide seagreen eyes and she wore nothing except her hair which was like a cloak, covering her down to her hips. It was lovely hair, shining and rippling in the light of the rising moon.

Mick, who was a postman after all, and understood difficult things like engines and bookkeeping, just stared. "Who—what are you?" he said.

Matt, who didn't understand engines or bookeeping, told him, "She's a mermaid."

"I'm glad *somebody* around here has a little education," said the mermaid crossly.

"What's your name?" asked Matt. "What were you doing so near land?"

"My name is Marina. I'm sick of the sea. Any chance of a job around here?"

"You need legs for a job," said Mick.

But Matt cut in, "Don't mind him. There are lots of jobs for people in wheelchairs."

Mick thought for a while. "I have a plan," he said. "Mammy had a wheelchair after she fell down the stairs and it's still up at our house. Marina can do Noreen's work. She can sit in the wheelchair and sell stamps."

"What are stamps?" asked Marina.

"You stick them on letters."

"What are letters?"

"They are messages you send through the post."

"Why do you do that?"

"Never mind. We'll explain all that later." They rolled up the net and stowed it away, and Mick took off his gansey and helped Marina to put it on.

"I like it," she said, "It smells of fish."

Then Mick fetched the green van with *An Post* painted on its side and they crammed Marina into the back. She was awkward to move about because she didn't bend much in the middle where her tail started.

All the people of the village had gone to Dingle so as to sell the bass at first light. There was nobody about at the post office. They carried Marina indoors, switched on the light and discovered that her lovely long hair was seaweed green. "*Now* what?" said Mick. "Whoever heard of a post office assistant with green hair?"

"Why not?" said Matt. "I've seen girls on the telly with green hair, pink hair, blue hair and no hair at all. "We'll say she's a pop singer on holiday."

"That's a great idea," said Mick. "Marina, can you sing?"

"Of course I can. All mermaids sing." And she began to sing in a liquid silvery voice.

"That's fine, now hush; someone will hear. What would you like for supper?"

"A piece of bass will do if there's any left." said Marina.

"Would you like a cup of tea?"

"I'll try anything once," she said. "Put plenty of salt in it, will you."

"Salt?"

"Yes. I never drank anything but salt water until now."

Mick and Matt spent the whole night teaching Marina how to sell stamps for letters and postcards, how to stick them on, how to give change. She learned quickly, but she couldn't read, which made it hard for her.

"It's lucky it's holiday time," said Matt. "I can help her on the quiet."

When it got light, Marina wound and coiled and plaited all her beautiful green hair and put it up on top of her head. She fastened it with fishbones. She looked very beautiful, sitting in the wheelchair in Mick's navy gansey.

"What'll we do about the bottom half?" asked Matt.

They searched their mother's wardrobe, and at last they found the very thing—a long tweed skirt; the sort that wraps around and is fastened with a pin. They fastened it around Marina, and it was just long enough to cover the end of her tail.

She ate a tin of sardines for breakfast, and drank a cup of coffee with lots of salt.

Mick had to go off with the post, and he told Matt whatever happened to remember the story they had made up. Marina was a pop singer from Donegal who was in a car accident and who had lost all her money. So she had taken a summer job and was only learning the way of it.

The first person to visit the post office that day was Mrs Kitty Kelly, the most inquisitive woman in Kerry. She fired one question after another at Marina, and Matt answered most of them for her. "She's shy," he explained to Kitty.

"Shy! A shy pop singer! That's a good one! I don't believe a word of it. Have you broken your leg dear?"

"Worse than that," said Marina, sadly.

"Well, I suppose you were lucky that your face wasn't marked—that is, if you mean to go on singing," said Kitty. "Of course, you might get a job in one of the guesthouses when you can get about again. Will it take long for the dye to wash out of your hair?"

"You're very rude," said Marina, turning red. "Where I come from, you'd be left sitting all night on a rock for that, with nothing to eat." Matt giggled, and Kitty flounced out, muttering to herself.

The next customer was a French tourist who wanted to know the proper postage for postcards going to France, Italy, Canada and Australia. Matt did some quick thinking, and decided that for the faraway places, the most expensive stamps they had would be right. The Frenchman put a £1 stamp on his postcard to Australia and went away grumbling.

"How are you enjoying it?" asked Matt. "You don't *look* very happy."

"I'm not, I'm too dry. Haven't you got a shower?"

"No, but there's a sprinkler thing you fasten on the kitchen tap."

So Marina wheeled herself into the kitchen, and showered herself until the gansey and the tweed skirt were soaked and there was a lake on the floor. Then

Mick arrived back from his round with the news that there was a post office inspector on his way from Tralee to see the girl who was doing Noreen's job.

"Quick! No time to lose!" Mick backed the van up to the kitchen door, and once again Marina was crammed inside. Matt was left to mind the post office, while Mick set off driving as fast as he could. Marina wriggled out of the skirt as they drove; the tweed had been rubbing against her scales and she hated it.

At last they reached a little cove near Ballyferriter. Mick was going to say goodbye and arrange to meet again, when he heard cars coming down the road. The inspector had seen the van, and following him were Kitty Kelly and her husband, while the tourist on a motorbike was close behind. Quick as a flash, Mick tipped Marina out of the van, and she rolled and rolled until she was in the sea. Then she dived, and that was the last Mick saw of her.

A few weeks later, when the evenings were getting chilly, a boatload of fishermen was cruising around Slea Head. When they got back to Dingle, they told their friends that they had seen a mermaid sitting on a rock singing.

"Extraordinary," said the friends.

"Yes," said the fishermen. "Whoever heard of a mermaid wearing a blue gansey?"

The Wizard's Sheep

ot so long ago, an old man lived in the woods in Co Wicklow. He was a strange old man—a wizard, some people said. He didn't care a pin for anybody, so nobody cared for him; he lived by himself because he liked his own company. He wore a raggy old jacket, one black welly and one green, and a cloth cap worn back to front. He had wispy grey hair and a little beard and sharp black eyes. His name was Con.

Con lived in the wildest part of the woods, by a waterfall. Here, the broad river swept to the edge of a crag and poured roaring over the side. You couldn't hear anything but the thunder of the wild water. At the foot of the waterfall, the grass grew lush and bright green.

Con didn't have visitors, but people who passed that way noticed that he had a flock of twenty sheep grazing there, and a black and white collie to mind them. Some said that there were never more or less than twenty ewes, that the thirty lambs running with them never grew any bigger, and that the dog which guarded them had done so for thirty years or more. Others said that this was nonsense.

Not far away from Con's house stood a ruined barn, and there a gang of sheep-stealers used to meet. There was Creepy Joe and Slippery Sam and Sneaky Sid and Cross-Eyed Chris. The other thief was called Hopeless Harry because he was so bad at stealing sheep.

Joe and Sam and Sid and Chris were sick of Harry. He nearly got them all caught several times, and he was caught himself and sent to prison. When he came out of prison, he found that the others didn't want him along any more. Harry begged and pleaded. He said he would try hard to be a better thief. (He had to learn the hard way—you can't take a course in sheep-stealing.)

"No," said the others, "we're sick of you. Go away and rob a bank." They thought that if Harry tried to rob a bank, he'd be caught and sent back to prison, perhaps for years. Then he wouldn't spoil their wicked plans.

Harry had a better idea. He thought he would steal Con's twenty sheep and their lambs. First of all, he decided to steal the black and white dog, then he would order the dog to round up the sheep and take them to a village where a dishonest friend of his owned a lorry. He told his friends about the plan and they agreed to divide the money when the sheep were sold.

Harry spent weeks working out his plan. He bought twelve tins of expensive dogfood. On the label was written, NO DOG CAN RESIST *HAPPIDOG*. Every day, Harry opened a tin of *Happidog* and crept up to the clearing where the dog stayed with the sheep, guarding them. "Glen, Glen," Harry would call quietly (the dog's name was Glen,) and Glen would come to him, licking his lips. Harry would put lumps of the meat on the ground, and Glen would creep forward, snatch the food and go back to his post, chewing it. Somehow, Harry could never catch hold of him—it was like trying to catch a puff of smoke.

One evening, as Harry was opening the eleventh tin of *Happidog*, he heard old Con calling. Harry lay flat in the bracken and listened. Con shouted, "Hey, Glen boy, bring 'em in. Bring 'em in, Glen boy—get back there." Then he whistled three times. Glen looks wistfully in the direction of the tin of food, but he galloped off obediently, rounded up his sheep and drove them away out of sight. Harry heard Con saying, "Good lad, Glen, Good lad."

That night, Harry went to a lonely place on the Wicklow Gap, and there he practised and practised copying Con's voice and his whistle. At last he was satisfied, and he went home to bed. When he was in bed, the soles of his feet and the middle of his back itched and kept him awake. This was because old Con had seen him hiding in the bracken. Con really *was* a wizard and knew where he was and what he was up to. Harry was too far away for Con to hurt him with his spells, but the tickling was most annoying, and he couldn't reach the middle of his back to scratch it. Con lay in his grubby old feather bed and laughed and laughed as he thought how he would deal with Harry.

Harry didn't take a tin of *Happidog* with him the next night: he took a bicycle and left it behind a tree on the roadside. Then he inched his way towards the clearing. He heard the sheep tearing at the short grass and a lamb bleating. Harry's heart pounded. He tried to pitch his voice low and hoarse like Con's. "Hey, Glen boy, bring 'em in. Bring 'em in, Glen boy—get back there!" Then Harry whistled three times. At once he heard the clippety-clopping of twenty sets of small hooves, and the pitter-pattering of thirty sets smaller still. The sheep were all round him in a moment, Glen grinning behind them.

Delighted, Harry ran to the road and grabbed his bike. He had a hard time getting on to it, as the sheep pressed around him, baaing loudly. At last he was mounted, and set off, pedalling as fast as he could. But, fast as he rode, Glen drove the sheep faster; they galloped all round the bike, bleating as loud as they could.

Harry began to get really worried when he reached the village. There was something going on in the square—step dancing, he thought—but he didn't dare stop. Two gardai were standing by their squad car, watching. Harry's feet flew round as if he was training for the Tour de France. He raced through Manor Kilbride and past the lakes at Poulaphouca, feeling as if his lungs would burst.

On level ground, he gained on the sheep, and when he reached a long downhill stretch, he left them behind. Harry decided to ride to Blessington, catch a bus to Naas, and go on to Dublin the next day. Con could keep his sheep. Harry rode along, happier now except for a fierce itching in the backs of his legs.

Blessington was quiet: the bus was due in ten minutes. Harry thought he had time for a drink before it arrived, so he went into a pub, leaving his bike in the yard at the back. He gulped a pint of beer and went out. The sheep were packed tight around his bicycle, and Glen lay panting beside them.

When Harry appeared, Glen rounded up the sheep and drove them towards him. Harry shouted, "Lie down!" and "Go home!" It was no good. He went back into the pub, and the drinkers at the bar turned and stared. Close behind Harry trotted twenty ewes with their lambs. They ran straight down the bar, skidding on the slippery floor, and pushed their way through the swing doors at the far end, followed by a black and white collie.

Meanwhile, Harry had run to the bus

stop. The bus hadn't arrived, and he wondered if Glen would be able to chivvy the sheep into it. Hardly—but it wasn't worth risking. He raced back (with his escort) to the pub yard, jumped on his bike and away he went.

It was getting dark when two men from the *Society for Prevention of Cruelty to Animals* overtook a flock of sheep on the Naas bypass. The officials were driving a van: but of course no sheep are allowed on the motorway—or bicycles either for that matter.

The two men drove alongside, wondering. A black and white collie was taking the sheep along at full speed—but they weren't panting. The lambs were keeping up with them easily. The man who they supposed to be the owner was cycling ahead of them as if devils were after him. He kept looking behind him, he was gasping for breath and wobbling from side to side. "This looks more like cruelty to cyclists than to animals," said one of the men.

Now it is easier to get a flock of sheep on to a motorway than off it again. They all stopped at a lay-by, and the men asked Harry what he meant by treating his dog and his sheep so badly. He said that neither Glen nor the sheep were his, but the men didn't believe him. All three tried to catch Glen, but he slipped through their fingers every time. The sheep lay down to rest and the two officials made Harry get into their van where they asked him a lot of questions. When they next looked out, both dog and sheep had vanished.

Harry had to pay a fine, but as neither the animals nor their owner could be found, it was only for breaking laws on the motorway, not for stealing. He was so tired and so frightened that he went and looked for an honest job the very next day. The only job to be had was in a dogfood factory, and there you can see Harry to-day, sticking labels on tins of *Happidog*. He hates the work, but he has never been tempted to steal a single tin.

The morning after Harry took old Con's sheep, the gang were wondering how he'd got on. So Slippery Sam and Creepy Joe, Sneaky Sid and Cross-Eyed Chris went quietly to the clearing in the woods. There were all the sheep, grazing away, and the black and white collie watching them. "I knew Harry'd never get them away," said Sid.

"I wouldn't mind owning that dog," said Sam.

"Nor I," said Joe, "But he's well-known round here, we'd be caught if we took him."

"The old man feeds him well," said Sam, "Look!" Under the bushes where they were hiding, were eleven empty tins of *Happidog*.

The Bad-Tempered Prince

p and down the banks of the Shannon stand the ruins of castles. They used to be the homes of powerful lords and princes. That was in the days when the river was used as a highroad, and the real roads were just muddy sheep-tracks.

Some of the ruins have been rebuilt by the Tourist Board. Their towers are repaired and have spiral stone staircases inside them, and arrow slits in the walls. Sometimes, there is a notice on the wall, saying who lived there. Other castles have crumbled into piles of stones—nobody remembers who lived in them.

Right on the Shannon bank, somewhere

in Co Offaly, stands all that is left of a big square castle and, fifty yards away, all that is left of a small square tower. The king, who was called Cormac, lived in the big tower with his wife, Queen Bertha.

The king and queen had only one child, a little boy called Neil. They were quite elderly when Neil was born, and had been hoping in vain for a baby for twenty years. As a result, they spoiled him dreadfully.

From the start, Neil had a bad temper. At his christening in Clonfert, he yelled and howled until his face turned purple. "That's a good sign—it's the devil coming out," said Cormac. Just then Neil gave a wriggle and a twist and kicked the bishop on the nose. So Queen Bertha told off his godmother for not holding him tightly enough.

When Neil was six months old, he bit his old nurse's finger to the bone in a fit of rage. Nurse screamed, slapped him and ran to tell the Queen. Bertha took the shrieking baby in her arms and rocked him, taking no notice of Nurse's bleeding finger. "Poor little fellow, he's teething," she said.

Nurse was used to spoiled children, but Neil was something else. As he got older, he would lie on the floor and chew holes in the matting if he didn't get what he wanted. The only way that Nurse could carry him without being kicked or bitten was under her arm, face down, his head sticking out at the back and his feet at the front. When he grew too heavy for this, she gave notice.

Neil refused to go to school at the monastery, so kind Brother Luke came to the castle to teach him. Brother Luke soon found out that he couldn't teach Neil anything—not even how to read and write. The good Brother was a patient man and, when Neil threw the inkpot at him, he said, "I won't punish you because I know you didn't mean it."

"I *did* mean it," said Neil, and he dropped a live frog down Brother Luke's back.

So Brother Luke complained to the

Queen and she said, "Neil is excitable and high spirited. You must try to be more patient with him."

Brother Luke thought and thought. Then he remembered hearing that music was good for soothing bad-tempered people. So he persuaded King Cormac to hire a musician to play the bagpipes under Neil's window. Neil opened the window and threw a bucket of water over him. However, the musician had been promised a lot of money, so he moved out of reach and went on playing. Neil ran downstairs, grabbed the bagpipes and threw them into the river. Then the piper began to sing and Neil threw him into the Shannon after his pipes.

King Cormac said that Neil was right— the piper had been playing out of tune, but Brother Luke was angry and went back to his monastery.

By the time Neil was twenty years old, his rages were so awful that nobody wanted to live with him. Then King Cormac built him a little castle of his own at the end of the courtyard, and Neil went and lived there all by himself. The cook took him his meals, arriving with an armed bodyguard in case Neil didn't like the look of his dinner.

The King and Queen worried because Neil was their only son and they thought he should get married. But no girl would have dreamed of marrying him, although one day, his wife would be queen.

One day, as Neil sat fishing from the river bank, he saw a beautiful girl riding by. She was mounted on a coal-black horse, and her gold bracelets and necklaces clinked as she rode. She wore a scarlet cloak and, on her head, a gold circlet which flashed in the sun.

"Who do you thing you are?" Neil asked rudely. "Why are you dressed like a princess?"

"Because I *am* a princess. I am Princess Susanna from Galway. You aren't very good at fishing are you?"

Neil sprang up in a rage, and broke his fishing-rod in two—then he saw that

Susanna was laughing at him. "I'll teach you to laugh at me!" he yelled, grabbing at her horse's reins. Susanna swung the black around at the last second, so that its shoulder bumped against Neil and he tumbled headlong into the water. The she rode away, laughing.

Neil climbed dripping out of the Shannon. He thought of sending his soldiers to find Susanna and fetch her back, but he had a feeling that she might make a fool of him again.

When Neil complained to his father about Princess Susanna, he got a lecture for his pains. The princess was known throughout the length and breadth of Connacht. She had been tricked out of a kingdom by her stepmother and had no home of her own. Beaten by her father, hated by her stepmother, she had grown up a wild, lonely girl with a terrible temper. She could ride any horse and do anything she turned her hand to. She despised boys because they were afraid of her, and would do whatever she told them to. She had heard about Neil and thought he might be interesting. Now she had gone.

In the weeks that followed, Neil kept hoping that Susanna would come back, so that he could pay her back for pushing him into the river. When she did return, she was riding a different horse—milk white this time, and brought with her a pack of hounds, half a dozen servants and a spare horse. She invited Neil to go hunting, almost politely.

Neil was a good rider, and thought he would be able to impress Susanna, so he agreed. The horse was a handsome chestnut, and soon he was galloping along beside Susanna, delighted with hinself. They jumped over a fallen tree and Neil's horse stumbled, so he shouted angrily, "Hold up, you clumsy brute!" and hit it as hard as he could.

Susanna had been thinking that perhaps Neil wasn't so bad after all, but she loved her horses and had trained them herself. She blew a silver whistle and shouted, "Down!" and Neil's horse stopped and lay down like a dog. As she passed, she bent down and snatched the whip out of Neil's hand, then she cantered away. Nothing would make the horse get up again and the servants, trying not to laugh, refused to help, so Neil had to leave it lying there and walk home, feeling very foolish indeed.

This time, he decided to be very polite and well-behaved when Susanna came back—but she didn't come back. A whole year passed, and he was sure he was in love with her. He wandered about looking miserable, and even wrote a poem about her. Then he heard that she was to be married to the king of Sligo, which threw him into such a passion that he went hungry for a week; nobody dared to take him any food.

Neil thought that, if he couldn't marry Susanna, he might become a monk, so off he went to the monastery. But when the monks saw him coming, biting his nails and grinding his teeth, they gathered their few belongings and hurried away. So Neil had the whole place to himself, and very lonely it was.

One day, when Neil was digging potatoes for his dinner, Susanna rode into the courtyard. "I've been looking for you everywhere," she said, angrily.

"Why?" asked Neil. "I thought you'd married the King of Sligo."

"Oh no," said Susanna, "He's boring. 'Yes, dear, no dear, whatever you say, dear—' He agreed with everything I said. He'd have driven me mad in a week."

"Will you marry me instead?" asked Neil. "I promise never to agree with you."

"All right," said Susanna. "I think we suit each other perfectly."

So they got married and they fought all the time. They didn't have any friends, but they were too busy quarrelling to notice. And if they didn't live happily ever after, at least they were never bored.

The Turf Cutter's Donkey

and

Brogeen Follows the Magic Tune

by Patricia Lynch

"Classics of Irish Children's Literature"

Irish Independent

POOLBEG

Irish Sagas and Folk Tales

by Eileen O'Faoláin

Here is a classic collection of tales
from the folklore of Ireland

POOLBEG

The Poolbeg Book of
Children's Verse

Edited by Sean McMahon

A sparkling miscellany of poems for the
young and everybody else.

"Already a classic,"
RTE Guide

POOLBEG